The Glitter Keeper

The Glitter Keeper

A Story About Fitting In and Standing Out

by

Stacey Lytle

Copyright © 2016 by Stacey Lytle

www.StaceyLytle.com
Contact: LytleMomma@gmail.com

Edited by Jerusha Smith
jerusha@kat4.com

Illustrations by Danielle Powell
daniellepowellart@gmail.com
Instagram: @daniellepowellart

Layout and Design by Tyler Penner
www.typennerdesign.com
typennerdesign@gmail.com

First Printing, 2016
A Lytle of This & A Lytle of That Publishing, LLC
PO Box 1876
Eagle, Idaho 83616

ISBN-13: 978-0998418117
ISBN-10: 0998418110

Dedication

The Glitter Keeper is dedicated first to my dear husband, Chad . . . my Rock, my Happy Place, my Knight in Shining Armor, my Everything . . . Your constant belief in me and encouragement to follow my heart, while living life to the fullest, has helped me become who I am today. Thank you for making me laugh every day and for giving me endless reasons to be blissfully happy! I adore you!

And to that beautiful handful-and-a-half of kids that I'm so grateful to call, "mine . . ."

Shealyn, Danielle, Myles, Bryce, Wyatt, Cassandra and Natalie:
YOU have made every.single.day of being your mom an absolute crazy adventure and a pure joy!

My hope and prayer for each of you is that you will always stay true to who you are, that you will worry little about fitting in and forever remember that you were born into this world to STAND OUT and to make a beautiful difference for those around you. I am hopeful that you will fall in love with life, find wonder and awe in all miracles that surround you and above all else--my wish is that you will forever know that of all the things I could ever do in life, YOU have always been and will always be the most important. YOU are my treasures, at the top of the list of my favorite things, and the sparkling glitter of my life! XOXOXOX! Love, your Momma

And finally . . .

to the 16-year-old little girl in me that dreamed of writing and publishing books for children . . . yet, sat in her desk filled with fear of her future and doubt in herself, pushing those dreams away, believing dreams only happen for other people . . .

We did it!!!

It may have taken over three decades to muster up the courage, but that beautiful dream is now a fantastic reality. I believe in you--thank you for always believing in me and never giving up the hope for those dreams and those stories.

Hi! Hello! Hey, Friend!

I'm so glad you've come to sit for a spell!

I'm Trudy, and I'm delighted to be spending some time with YOU!!!

Why don't you get comfy? You might even wish to grab a scrumptious cup of cocoa and a cozy blanket to wrap up in while I share a wonderful story with you.

I've always dreamed of starting a story out with just a few of my favorite magical words . . . Ready? Here we go!!!

1

"Once upon a time . . ."

Ohhhhh, I *love* that! Reading those four little words fills me with thoughts of great imagination and joy!

Okay, for real this time—the whole story:

Once upon a *fanciful* time, not so very long ago, there was an extraordinary place that few have ever had the pleasure of visiting. In this place lived an enchanting, extra-tiny she-elf who went by the name of, "Trudy." Yep, this is my story!

Isn't this fun?

Let's keep going . . .

I want to tell you everything!

My story is one of those very happy and very sad stories all wrapped up in one perfect little package, and tied off with the bounciest bow you could imagine! Go ahead, imagine it . . . isn't it spectacular?

If you haven't already guessed, I live at the North Pole. In fact, I'm the very smallest she-elf in all of Santa's workshop, and let me tell you, there's a gob of us here! And all of those dazzling things you've heard about the North Pole? They are true! Santa's Workshop is truly magical!

Have you ever experienced something magical? Wonderful? Positively and utterly fantabulous? So crazy-amazing that it hardly feels like it could really be happening??

I have!

That's exactly what it's like at the North Pole! All of the elves are busy, busy, busy . . . busy happily building and preparing toys and gifts for children all over the world! There is always something magnificent happening in Santa's workshop!

Santa joins us every single afternoon with a booming, cheerful, "Ho, Ho, Ho!" as he passes out the most delightful hot cocoa and fresh cookies! Some days we have scrumptious chocolate chip, other days decadent snicker-doodles or beautifully frosted sugar cookies with sprinkles . . . Every once in a while, Mrs. Claus tries out a new cookie recipe to see what we think of it. We always cheer for her new, delectable creations—they never disappoint us! I believe it's because they're made with love. Each and every day, they are positively perfect, and the scent of fresh cookies lingers in the workshop; that time of the day is probably my most favorite of all!

There was one day, though, when Santa didn't join us. I kept waiting—he always came! It was hard to accomplish much when every few seconds I would find myself looking at the front doors of the workshop, waiting for Santa's grand entrance.

Santa's Head-Elf, Theodore, went to the front of the room after lunch, and stood on top of the very highest stool in the workshop to get our attention. Clearing his throat nervously, it was plain to see he was shaking in his boots! Theodore was such a gentle giant of an elf—he had a heart of solid gold and wished to keep everyone as happy as possible. He appreciated cheer and merriment more than any other elf, except maybe me (I lived for it)!!!

It was hard for me to see him feeling so nervous and vulnerable. In that moment, I wished I could run to his side to share a touch of encouragement with him. I knew exactly how he felt—standing there, with all eyes on him. I knew it could feel so terrifying (it could make you want to hide behind the tallest pile of wrapping paper) . . . what if no one laughed when you hoped they might? Or, worse yet, what if they laughed at you when you least expected it? I was kind of used to that . . . I did my best, but I often felt my cheeks turn hot with embarrassment as others giggled at my silly, out-of-the-ordinary actions.

I had to do something for Theodore . . . I jumped up and down, waving my arms wildly in an attempt to grab his attention. Once our eyes met, I gave him my best thumbs-up along with a twinkling wink! He snickered and smiled. I noticed a slight pinkening of his cheeks as he confidently sucked in a rejuvenating breath, lifted his shoulders, and rang one of Santa's sleigh bells to address us. "I have some news to share with you! Please gather around . . . quickly, now . . . we've not any time to waste!" He paused and then continued, "Please don't be alarmed, but Santa is not well." Worried chatter filled the room. He rang the sleigh bell again and after some whispering died out, all was quiet. He went on, "Santa has come down with a nasty cold—his body is terribly feverish and he has chills. Not to worry though! Mrs. Claus is tending to his every need. She has a crackling fire blazing, and has him tucked comfortably in his bed with extra coverings drawn all the way up to his chin, along with a giant mug of her piping hot cocoa for him." He let out a small chuckle and went on to reassure the elves, "Truly, there is no need to worry! She will fuss over him until he is good as new—but it may take some time."

9

Again, the room filled with murmuring and concern. Theodore continued and the room was hushed a third time. "In the meantime, Santa has asked that we bring in a supervisor to take over while he is away. It is essential that we keep toy production going. We all know about the All-Important Day that is fast approaching, and we must be prepared! Santa could not bear the thought of disappointing a single child!"

With that, Theodore, drew in another deep breath—he seemed more uncomfortable than ever. "I've searched high and low, near and far, to find someone to fill Santa's role in the workshop. This was no easy assignment, I might add. It was unbelievably difficult because elves that I spoke to are already too busy with their current duties. I met with all of the Keepers of the Reindeer; then on to the schoolhouse—but no luck there, either. Just as I was thinking there wasn't another un-busy elf in the entire North Pole, I met someone that I would like to introduce to you. Please welcome . . . Sebastian!" From behind the nearby wall, emerged "Sebastian." He easily stood an extra two—or maybe three—feet higher than the very tallest elf in the workshop. His body was spindly, with pointed elbows and knees. His face seemed to be positioned in a permanent frown; in fact, I felt certain that if a smile tried to sneak across his face, it would run the risk of cracking his entire head! I gasped, and then did my best to cover it up with a little cough.

Sebastian was undeniably stern and strict as he demanded our attention. His expression was—and stayed—as still as stone. The workshop became silent instantly—no one knew Sebastian, or what he would do or say. Where had he been working at the North Pole? Why had we never seen him before? He certainly would've been hard to miss. His unfriendly tone of voice was short and blunt as he—with no emotion—told us, "Santa will be away for quite some time. You are to give him his space, am I understood?" We all nodded without making a sound—we were still scared. "You are to report to me," Sebastian barked out. "The priority and only focus of this workshop will be production, production, production! There is no time for fun and games and I will not tolerate it! I work best with quiet, and so would all of you, if you tried it!" Sebastian went on to explain that there would be no "extras" for projects—nothing fancy added to the toys, and no frills!

As he finished, I raised my hand . . . I realize now that was a BIG mistake!

"Excuse me . . . um, Mr., uh—Supervisor, Mr. Sebastian? Will we be enjoying our cocoa and cookies today?"

With a grumble and a loud "harrumph," he turned away. It was obvious we would not be enjoying *anything*, if Mr. Sebastian had his way. Elves began to murmur to each other, but were quickly put in their place as Sebastian shot a look across the room that was as chilling and harsh as the howling North Winds during the most biting of storms. Silence was again instantaneous, and Sebastian quickly departed through the front doors of the workshop.

Over the next several days, the elves in Santa's workshop quickly adjusted to a new, subdued feeling while they worked. I, however, struggled. How do you give away everything that makes you who you are? How could I not sing and dance and add special touches to my work? Santa had always seemed to love these sorts of things. Sebastian, on the other hand, loathed it!

I just waited for the day that Santa's health would return, and he would feel well enough to start visiting us again. Meanwhile, I did my very best to not cause any commotion or problems for Sebastian—or *anyone* else.

I was known for drawing all sorts of unwanted attention my way. The other elves often felt frustrated or bewildered by me. Some seemed to like me if I was the only one they had to talk to, and a few giggled whenever I was around—I've never known if that meant that they liked me or not. A couple of the elves—like Theodore—always like me even when I'm at my zaniest! But the rest . . . I don't think they like me one single bit, maybe I frighten them with all the bursts of energy that find a way of springing out of me . . . I don't really know . . .

Remember that I mentioned that this is a happy and sad story all mixed up? Well, life at the North Pole didn't *always* feel magical or wonderful or fantabulous . . . In fact, you might even describe some days as feeling like a few of the loneliest, saddest, letting-down-iest kind of days ever! At least, that is how it felt some of the time for me.

Have you ever wanted someone to like you? Have you ever wished you could just fit in? Maybe be like everyone else? Not stick out in a crowd? Or—even worse—feel totally invisible in a room? Have you ever longed for a friend or two who just understood you?

If you have, I know exactly how you feel!

The truth is . . . I just didn't fit in. I wasn't like the others . . . and many of the elves made sure I knew they didn't like it.

Sometimes, I felt completely invisible and unnoticed, and other times I felt like the class clown . . . big red nose, floppy shoes, and all!

I was too much for some of the elves—and never enough for the others.

I looked different, I acted differently, I felt differently, I even thought different, crazy thoughts. Yeah, it's totally true!

It showed in everything about me,

from my bright, mismatched clothes,

to my droopy hat with the wild dingle-berry-puffball on top,

all the way down to the big, sparkly shoes that rarely stayed put on my feet.

It's always easy to pick *me* out of crowd.

Some–like Santa–say that's a good thing . . . he's shared that it's important to be unique–to be exuberant and ever-inquisitive. I'm not so sure I agree with him. Maybe he doesn't realize that it's pretty hard being so unlike everyone else.

Everything about me seems to scream out, "Look at me, I'm different! I'm not at all like anyone else!"

 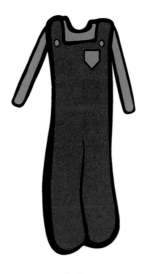 

I started paying close attention to those around me, and guess what I noticed? All of the other elves seemed content with wearing matching clothes, but I simply could not see the appeal of wearing red and green, day in and day out . . . I truly have to wonder—have the others not noticed the fantastic rainbow of colors to choose from? Can't they see how much happier bright colors might feel? I seem to be the only one. I've put on those reds and greens, I really have, but you know what happens?

Absolutely nothing . . .
nothing special at all . . .
I just feel "blah . . ."

 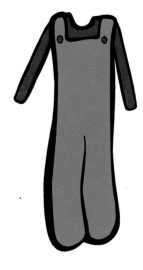 

. . . *but,* when I put on my *spectacular* yellow dress that has the darling blue and green polka-dots, with the fancy frills hanging from the edges, along with my periwinkle-purple and bubblegum-pink striped leggings, coupled with one of my favorite sparkly sets of shoes—and I throw in a super-cute hat—just for FUN . . .

. . . I feel I can do ANYTHING!

That's the magic of wearing clothes that you love!

Oh, and one more thing about how I always "stand out": even if I *was* wearing the red and green, I have *this* hair! Even from the time I was just a teeny-tiny she-elf, my hair was everywhere! Curly locks of pink, red, and blonde—with shimmering pockets of sparkling silver and gold—dance about my face and cascade to the small of my back.

All of the other elves—they have behaving hair . . . you know, the kind that just stays as it should and is only one color? Hair that doesn't feel the need to dance and practically shout with every move of the head?

Their *hats* even behave, fitting ever so nicely atop their well-mannered hair! Mine can be seen hanging on for dear life as my curls shift this way and that! That hat of mine is forever sliding clear down my colorful mop of curls and landing with a "plop" at my feet. I can't even say that I blame it—it really must be thoroughly and utterly exhausting trying to contain such excited, untamed hair!

I have to tell you, I've tried—TRULY tried—to fit in and make friends. I put myself in the middle of things time after time after time! I didn't smash myself up against the wall pretending to not be there (even though I often wanted to do that), and I did my *best* to find a place to belong.

I remember one day, I invited some of the other elves over to see something I was so happy about! In my spare time—a little second here and a little moment there—I was able to build a dreamy little sunroom that allowed streaks of sunlight to radiate in and fill every pocket of an old storage room. This was a day I had long-anticipated, and the time was finally right—everything was perfect!

Scattered along the shelves and hanging from baskets of all sizes grew the most stunning flowers! I had one for almost every letter of the alphabet. I had cared for and nurtured these beauties since they were the tiniest of seedlings . . . The scents that filled the room delighted my nose each morning, and their bright buds made me bubble over with joy! In this special room of mine grew everything from African Daisies, Balloon Flowers, Blazing Stars, and Buttercups to Coral Bells and Daffodils! The Forget-Me-Nots, Gerber Daisies and Honeysuckle blossoms were a few of my favorites. Oh, and the Lady's Slipper and Lilacs were a treat! Moon Flowers and Sunflowers along with the most delicately shaped Wish-Makers—known to most as dandelions or weeds—always made my heart want to dance in my chest! To top it all off, and bring the alphabet to a close, were the Snapdragons, Snow*drops* and Snow*flakes*, Tulips, Violets, Water Lilies and Wallflowers, along with Whirling Butterflies and Zinnias.

I had waited for this day for so long, I was positively giddy! I knew all of the elves would love it just as much as me . . . but, at the end of the day, I had to love all of those beautiful flowers enough for everyone, because everyone thought having a greenhouse at The North Pole was silly and totally out of place. They shook their heads in disbelief. *Why would I waste my time doing something so unnecessary?* They wanted to know. "Of all the nonsense! Flowers! And there's so much to do!" Muttered Humphrey, still holding his hammer from his workstation. I even overheard him whisper to Fitzgerald—a block-painting elf—"Elves are supposed to like snow and ice and pine trees . . . not flowers and sunshine and make-believe springtime! Why does Trudy have to be so different from the rest of us?"

My heart dropped a little,
but those bright blooms had a way of picking me right back up!

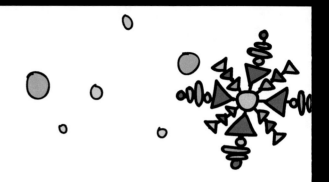

There were times I felt really confused and disappointed. I tried to be like the other elves. I even tried to hide the real me, because the ME that I was just wasn't quite right.

Sure, I like the snow and icicles—I'm an elf, after all! When the snowflakes fall, I am generally the first one outside, tongue sticking out, twirling in circles, doing my best to catch a mouthful. And if you are lucky enough to catch one on the end of your finger and *really* check it out, they are a sight to see—each with its own beauty, shape and size. But, isn't it okay to also love all of the other seasons? If you ask me, it's sad and disappointing that spring and summer don't grace the North Pole. I can scarcely envision autumn—the rich sensation of fiery colors exploding on all of the trees. I am a tad peculiar—always curious about what the rest of the world is able to see and enjoy. The other elves just don't seem to care all that much about anything but the North Pole . . .

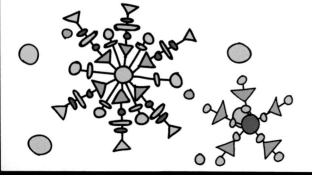

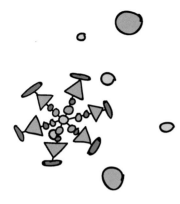

It seemed that I was always sticking out and seldom fitting in with the rest of the elves, but it had felt overwhelmingly so this year while Santa was ill and unable to visit the workshop for so long. Oh, how I missed his merry laugh! He had a way of making things come to life like no one else! And he seemed to "get me" . . . being me was pretty okay when he was around. With him gone, I stuck out like the Sunflowers in my greenhouse—a flower at the North Pole that no one appreciated.

29

It was the busiest time in the workshop, and the elves had become quite serious and focused on the tasks at hand. They did just as Sebastian had instructed. I *tried* to be serious and stay focused, too. It wasn't all that easy for me . . . I'd catch myself skipping through the workshop whistling one of Santa's favorite songs, lost in the joy of all that was happening. What an exhilarating time of the year!!! I lived moment to moment, certain I would burst from all of the anticipation!!! I was eager to please, but since Santa had been ill, it seemed all that I had been doing was somehow causing others to feel grouchy. They just wished to get their work done—without all the happy fuss I caused.

I can't seem to help that I am forever drawn to every sparkling trinket or shiny gizmo that adorns the shelves of the workshop. The others are so right—I am an inquisitive little elf, to be sure! My exuberance and enthusiasm for life is not always welcomed, however, especially by the all-too-serious Supervisor. Sebastian always seems to be right around the corner when a burst of giggles wants to sneak out of me . . . His crabby face quickly makes any joyful moment melt away, and I pull myself together and try to act "appropriately."

It can be hard and lonely . . . sometimes I hear whispers and snickering around me. You know what I do? I just pretend the other elves are talking about a different Trudy instead of me! Yep, it helps . . . at least a little. When I do that, I can keep my best cheerful face on and keep doing things my way—the way that makes me happiest. This was working pretty well for me . . .

. . . pretty well, that is, until one day—a day that will surely go down in Elf History . . .

I was positively certain it was the very *worst* day in Elf History, too.

For me, it was the day that changed everything.

It started with this ahhhhhh-mazing shelf tucked away in the corner! It had always been my biggest favorite! Oh, how I yearned for the beauty it held! It was a shelf that no one ever went to anymore—I don't know why. Over time, it had accumulated a blanket of dust, but even through that layer, it was clear that it was filled with sparkling containers. Jars of glitter, bottles of buttons of every shape and size, as well as sequins, gemstones, and even ribbons of all colors cascading down in tendrils. The most stunning of the shiny knick-knacks, doo-hickeys and thingamajigs in the workshop sat on this inviting shelf.

I had been intensely focused on the job of painting the cabooses at my station; I'd even turned my stool away from facing *that* shelf. The temptation was too great for an elf such as myself.

I remember nearly pleading with my craft brush to behave, for it took on a life of its own as I painted—it always had. I tried with all of my might to keep it from mixing paint colors. The caboose was to be entirely red—I'd been talked to about this before—just recently, in fact! Sebastian was quick to notice me when I messed up . . . there were rules, and blending colors was not allowed! Neither was coloring outside the lines, but my brush and those paints just wished to rush together, almost begging to be swirled around, adding a swish of new color here and there . . .

Feeling exasperated,
        I turned away,
                just for a moment from my painting . . .

All of a sudden—before even paying attention to what I was doing—I had climbed all the way to the tippy-top of that old creaky, wooden ladder that rested precariously against *the shelf*!

I hadn't meant to climb up, and I hadn't meant to reach with all the stretchy-stretch-stretch I had in me . . . I really hadn't meant to use every last ounce of muster my itsy-bitsy body had to wiggle until my fingertips finally reached that great big, sparkling jar filled with glitter . . . Oh, how it twinkled! I am convinced my eyes lit up like never before as my mind raced with possibilities! The things I could create with such fantastic, colorful glitter were endless!

What happened next was terrible, and I had certainly NEVER meant for *it* to happen . . . and everyone was looking at me. At first, there was dead silence; not a single sound was heard.

I hadn't meant to let the glitter slip from my fingertips—I had only wanted to carry it down the ladder . . . but the lid toppled right off and the glitter showered over my head and onto the floorboards and ladder beneath me.

I stood as still as a Christmas tree, the empty jar still in my hands, keenly aware of the throbbing heartbeat in my chest that I could feel in my ears, and the feeling of tears choking at my throat . . . I secretly hoped no one would notice the mess I'd just created. I thought to myself, maybe, just maybe, no one saw . . . I know—wishful thinking, right?

Unfortunately, some did notice; to be specific—I'm sure everyone noticed! All of the elves throughout Santa's workshop began to laugh, and their laughter increased, getting louder and louder . . . Some were angry that I'd made such a mess, and others found it all quite funny. Now they had an even better reason to laugh at me. Some that I actually *thought* were my friends, joined in on the laughter . . . I was grateful to see that Theodore was not laughing, though. He stood in the corner, looking uncomfortable and sad; it seemed he didn't know what to do. The other elves weren't aware of him, however, and their voices continued. My heart felt like it was being shattered into a bazillion teeny-tiny little pieces, never to be reassembled the same way again.

Another goof-up on my part, and I felt like every elf at the North Pole had seen it . . . Their murmuring and jokes started, and I wished I would have just closed my eyes, plugged my ears, and sang out, "la-la-la-la-la," to cover it all up, because you can't un-hear things once you've heard them.

"How hard is it to just paint the train cabooses red, the engines blue, and all of the freight cars gray? Can't all elves follow simple directions?" Spouted Max, an elf nearest me. "Everyone seems to be able to, except for *Trudy*!"

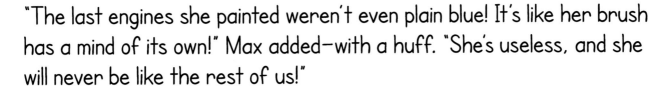

"I know," snickered Millie, a black-haired she-elf at another nearby table. "Why can't Trudy just do what she's supposed to? What a terrible mess she's made again! Sebastian is going to be so mad!"

"The last engines she painted weren't even plain blue! It's like her brush has a mind of its own!" Max added—with a huff. "She's useless, and she will never be like the rest of us!"

"Have you noticed her clothes? Of course, how could you miss them? They were crazy before, but now she's covered in glitter from head to toe! I'll bet that won't ever wash out of that untamed mop she calls 'hair'!" Chortled Maggie, a she-elf with blond hair, and a loud giggle.

"That's right! And that hat . . .WOW! She can't even seem to keep it on top of her head! Maybe the glitter will help it stick!" Taunted Millie as she giggled and pointed.

I trembled as I climbed down from the ladder to the floor, being careful to turn my head so that the others would not notice the trickling of tears on my flushed cheeks. My knees felt weak and wobbly, and they trembled as they tried to keep me up. I felt so heavy and so completely alone.

Try as I might to make order out of the mess that was scattered all over the floor . . . and ladder . . . and everywhere else nearby, my efforts seemed pointless. The glitter would not cooperate!

Then I remembered the words Santa had once said:

"*. . . glitter was never meant to be wiped away clean~glitter was meant to leave a bit of hope and brightness to share with all who might see it.*"

In my haste—and wrapped up in thoughts of Santa—I hadn't noticed the sudden hush of the workshop, until a set of feet steadily marching in my direction caught my full attention. There was a heavy drop of each foot as they approached, and all at once, shoes stood just to my side. I looked up, for what seemed like so many tick-tocks of the clock, and to my dismay, I encountered the gaze of my ever-stern Elf Supervisor, Sebastian. He didn't utter a word, but it was clear as I looked at his face that I had once again gained his disapproval. I missed Santa now more than ever! How I wished he could feel better and return to the workshop!

I drew in a deep breath, stood, and with a quivering voice I whispered, "I am so sorry! I—I—didn't mean to make a mess. I only wanted to make these gifts for the children more beautiful. What little girl wouldn't love ribbons, lace and glitter on her baby doll? And those buttons from the bottles, oh, they would have been the perfect additions to the caboose and engine cars! I didn't want such chaos—I just wanted to make the world a happier and shinier place."

I could see from his fierce eyes and frowning face that my ideas had no place here! He turned on his heels and marched away more quickly than he had come, leaving me wishing I could magically change everything back to the way it was before I had made this mistake. I knew I couldn't do that, but I suddenly wondered if I could at least hide—or somehow disappear!

That day in the workshop was the longest, most humiliating, most dreadful day that I had ever known in my little elf life. The snickering and comments continued . . . and I did my best to shut out all of the words that hurt.

"I sure hope Santa didn't see her, he would be so disappointed," murmured Maggie.

"Almost as disappointed as our Supervisor . . . he was fuming mad! Can you believe that Trudy doesn't listen to the new rules of the workshop?" Millie muttered.

"I wonder if she'll start walking around like the rest of us now, or if she'll keep up with all her skipping and cart-wheeling!" Max grumbled.

" . . . and all that noise she makes . . . whew! Maybe Sebastian is right. I'm thinking it sure would be nice to have some quiet to work in around here!" Sneered Maggie.

Dreadfully deflated, I wandered home that evening with a determination to never stand out again! I would do whatever I had to do to be *acceptable*, instead of a "mess-up."

First things first, I thought to myself: I safely tucked away all of my favorite items of clothing, including my fun hats and sparkly shoes.

Hesitantly, I then pulled out the red and green that so perfectly matched all of the other elves, and decided for certain in that moment I could learn to love fitting in and not being different anymore. *Wearing clothes you loved didn't matter that much, right?* I reasoned with myself. Red and green it would be, and I would be content with it.

But even as I tried to talk myself through this difficult moment, dinosaur-sized tears poured from my eyes. Inside my chest, it felt as though a huge, heavy rock was squishing my heart . . . my heart ached with a pain I had never known it could. I felt so sad, so empty, and I couldn't remember a time that I felt as awful as I did in that moment—not even when I spilled the glitter! All I wished to do was make my pain go away. There was no one who could understand what I was feeling. A broken heart, that's what I decided I had. It had to be broken, or it wouldn't hurt so much. I wondered if elves ever recover from being heartbroken, or if I'd stay this way forever.

Through the darkness of that night, I snuck into the workshop, knowing exactly what I needed to do. I pushed and pulled and heaved with all my might, panting and puffing away as I angled my elf-sized workstation to a different spot in the workshop. Then, looking around, I grabbed all of the most perfect items to meet my goal: a box or two would do quite well, along with a couple of books here, and a few building blocks there . . . In no time at all, I'd built a wall just high enough to block out all of the distractions of the workshop! Next, I removed all of the FUN things from my worktable, and tidied it up to be perfect—like the other workstations around mine. I wouldn't be needing glue or ribbons or lace, and I *certainly* wouldn't be needing ANY MORE GLITTER!

The next day, and the day after that and the day after that and the day after that . . . all of the elves stayed busy, busy, busy . . . Most of them hardly noticed the changes that I had made. I didn't think they cared. What I did think was that something was changing inside of me, and I didn't like it . . . but I wasn't sure what to do. I felt helpless, because I wanted people to like me and I wanted them to be happy with me.

It was like there was a tug-of-war going on inside me: two feelings battled to be in charge. One of them was Courage, and wanted to stick up for me—like Santa Claus . . . he wanted me to be my bubbly self and not be afraid of what others said about me that was unkind. The feeling fighting the Courage was Fear—a coward that acted like a bully; a lot like Sebastian and the elves that complained about me. This bully was determined and powerful and said everything was wrong with being the "Trudy" I knew, and kept pointing out everyone else and saying they were better than me.

I wonder why that awful bully feeling wins some days . . . when it does, I forget how much I like being the real me, and it's frustrating.

The only person I truly know how to be is Trudy. It's not fun feeling this way . . . why can't I just be me and not worry about it? But I did have to worry . . . didn't I?

Production was booming! Santa's workshop buzzed with work as Christmas was only eleven days away. There was little chatter, and music didn't fill the air as it once had. The toys were built just as they should be, and no big messes were made. No giggles were heard, and joy and merriment seemed to wither away and disappear.

Most of the elves seemed to be okay with the changes—the once wildly thriving workshop now more closely resembled a warehouse filled with robots. I certainly noticed it. At first, it felt stifling to me, but with time it became easier.

In the beginning, I had to stay focused, walking with my head held low, looking only at the floor—my fool-proof way of making it though Santa's workshop without getting too distracted. Oh, and that ahhhh-mazing shelf! I NEVER EVER walked or even *peeked* in that direction. After just a little time, something inside of me just didn't seem to care quite as much anymore about any of the things I used to love. The dancing didn't want to come from me, my songs seemed to be lost, and my wall did a very fine job of keeping my attention where it was meant to be— only on my work. I pumped out one red caboose after another; my brush didn't even have a close call with mixing colors anymore. My body that had once twirled and skipped and cart-wheeled through the workshop now quietly walked from one station to the other, with no whistling or humming trying to ring out. I had finally become just like the other elves: red *and* green *and* content.

Days that seemed like weeks passed . . .

The magic that was once so common diminished even further, leaving the workshop feeling absolutely gloomy.

I often wondered if anyone else felt the same sadness I felt. Didn't anyone else miss Santa's presence the way I did? My thoughts would often wander off, as painting an item the same color over and over and over took little concentration. I dreamed of the day that enchantment would once again fill the workshop, while also telling myself such dreams had no place in my life anymore.

Caught in my thoughts one day, I was startled when I suddenly realized—whispers and an actual thrilling feeling filled the room. The front doors of the workshop had just opened; I peered around my wall spotting a glimpse of the big shadow that now fell across the room. My eyes were drawn from the base of the shadow to the top of the figure that filled the doorway. It was Santa!!! What a treat!!!

Santa always had a way of bringing Magic and Cheer to the workshop! Oh my goodness, how I had missed him! Santa gently closed the doors behind him, and as all eyes watched, he made his way across the room; I had tucked my head safely back behind my wall. Something exciting had started to come alive in me, and I was so filled with the fluttering of old feelings—like Courage—that I feared at any moment I might bust out of my wall with joy! I squeezed my eyes shut tightly, trying to keep out all of the light possible, just waiting for this moment to pass so I could return to my work . . .

Are you ready for this??? This is my FAVORITE part of the story!!! Oh, what a terrifically Magical Day this turned out to be! Let's get back to it:

It was then that I sensed someone at my side. With my eyes still closed snuggly, my other senses seemed heightened. I noticed scents that made my nose tingle: there was a touch of chocolate-y cocoa, a hint of peppermint, and a woodsy-pine smell that made me want to draw closer. I lifted my eyelids only a little, just to have a teensy peek.

Kneeling before me was Santa Claus! My eyes rested just above his shiny black belt, and then gradually raised up and up and up, until finally meeting his warm gaze. I had never noticed his eyes before—they weren't like any others I'd seen. They seemed to dance and shimmer with happiness, much like the glitter I had spilled on the floor. In his eyes, I could see the reflection of my own. I noted how alike our eyes were—large teardrop eyes of emerald green—eyes that loved to be full of wonder. I continued to take in each feature of his face: his smile was contagious, his cheeks rosy, his round nose: a perfect fit for his sunny face, his beard: as white and soft as silk.

Santa reached for my hands and looked down at me with his merry eyes, and then shared the most beautiful message of hope with me:

"My dear Trudy, I have been watching you for some time. Yes, I saw you stand out for everyone in the workshop to see. I saw as you reached the tippy-top of the shelf to add that special touch of glitter to your creations. I smiled as the floor about you sparkled and twinkled. I noticed as the others laughed and pointed. I shed many tears as you piled the building blocks higher and higher about your workstation to shield yourself from everyone and everything around you. I cried as you tried to become someone you were never meant to be . . . Sweet child, you have such gifts to share with the world, yet you have chosen to hide the very things that make you unique—that make *you* sparkle and shine."

"Trudy, what do you wish? What do you dream? Do *those* things, for it is in doing those things that you will be your brightest, and a gift to those around you. It is in those things that you will find joy. Trudy, you are much like the glitter of the world—you are meant to dazzle and leave a bit of hope and beauty to share with all you meet . . . beauty that can never be swept away."

Santa gave one last encouraging squeeze to my tiny hands he had held so softly in his, shared a quick wink with one of his smiling eyes, and stood to address the many elves in his workshop who were awed and at silent attention.

"This workshop is too quiet—and much too clean! Where is all the merriment? I hear no singing and see no dancing. My workshop should be filled with all that makes one happy! Ho, Ho, Ho, Ho, Ho!!!! On this very special day, I appoint Miss Trudy to a new position: as my very Special Helper! Her title from today and henceforth shall be,

'The Glitter Keeper'!"

He turned his attention back to me, lifting me high for all in the workshop to see. It had been so long since I'd felt so thrilled to be alive. The day I dreamed of had come; enchantment had returned!!! Santa had returned!!! And it was okay to be me!!!

Santa spoke to me again with words that were blissful to my ears, "My dear Trudy, will you please return to spreading your glitter and brightness? It helps make this workshop all it was meant to be!"

To my pleasant surprise, all of the elves in the workshop clapped and cheered with great Christmas Spirit! Out of the corner of my eye, I spotted Theodore, Santa's Head-Elf. He was waving his arms and—you guessed it—he gave me his best thumbs-up accompanied by a jolly wink. He seemed as happy as I was to have Santa back. Well, *almost* as happy. I didn't see how ANYONE could be as happy as I was! My heart felt lighter than ever before.

That very day, I took down the walls that had confined me and that I had allowed to become my world. I adorned my workstation with all that was glittery—anything that I loved, even adding a little touch of "springtime" from my beautiful sunroom of flowers. I began to dream again . . . and guess what? There was a definite magic that filled Santa's Workshop again, because others began to do the same! I saw other elves find joy and happiness in being themselves. I even caught one doing a cartwheel after crawling down from *my favorite shelf!* The Special Something that had been missing was definitely back.

Every once in a while, I'd catch a glimpse of myself in the mirror in the distant part of the workshop, and what I noticed always made me smile! Santa *did* understand what it was like to be different from everyone else . . . there was only one Santa, and there was only one ME!

My eyes were bright and hopeful again! I allowed them to wander, to be captivated—and when I saw something that spoke joy to my heart, I would simply go—no second thoughts, no second-guessing myself. I would jump from that chair of mine and rush to grab this or that for one of my exciting creations . . . ideas freely flowing through my mind . . .

It was music to my ears to hear the whistle or hum of elves throughout the workshop, and see the flips and cartwheels that were now a common occurrence. And *My Shelf* . . . well, it became the favorite place of all in the workshop! And Sebastian—he was given a job he could love: he was in charge of polishing Santa's sleigh! And you know what? I caught a smile crossing his face, and his head didn't even crack open like I had been sure it would!

As joyful laughter and the jingling of music filled the walls of the workshop, I unpacked that box of all of my favorite clothes, and tossed the red and green out for good!

What happened that day is simple really:

I once again believed—in fantastic possibilities, and in myself.

That day I felt Courage again, and I danced and twirled with it! And I didn't even worry who was watching.

The End . . .

The Beginning of living "Happily Ever After!"

About the Author

As the head of Stacey Lytle's editing team, I have the great fortune of writing her bio:

Stacey has been an educator for over twenty years, working primarily with children and the youth. She has also spent much of that time homeschooling her own seven children, empowering women and youth, working on teacher development projects and parent education. She loves coordinating events of all sizes and is responsible for the formation of several learning cooperatives. Stacey is the author of an educator's book entitled FUNology, and is the Program Director of a large elective-day program for school-aged children.

Facts not on her resume: Stacey flies by the seat of her pants, loves her husband and children more than any event or credential she carries, and loves chocolate almost as much. She loves to skip through life with joy and try a little of anything and everything that has the possibility of fun and happiness for herself—and especially for others. She loves going on dates with her Knight in Shining Armor—her wonderful husband—who is wise enough to know that taking her out for a milkshake in her "yellow slug-bug convertible" is one of her favorite things to do. (She also loves jumping out of said convertible at spontaneous moments to take a snapshot of the random sunflower, sunset, or dilapidated barn. We think the convertible has gotten used to it, and so has Stacey's family . . . mostly.)

Speaking for those of us that support Stacey in her offering of this magical tale of Christmas to the world, I can confidently say that who Stacey is is even more important to us than what Stacey does. If she had one wish come true, it would come before all of the presenting, organizing and speaking she has done: she would cover the whole world with glitter hoping it would give others the joy and love she feels for her family and for her life. Stacey is grateful for every day to be who she is, and those who read this story, we believe, will be grateful, too.

Jerusha Smith

About the Illustrator

Danielle Powell—born and raised in the San Francisco Bay Area—decided at a young age to pursue art. In middle school, she began drawing small portraits, in the simple hopes of developing a new hobby. Guided by her high school art teacher, Danielle quickly became interested in sculpture and aspired to learn more. After high school, she continued her education into the studio arts at Brigham Young University-Idaho, where she trained in various mediums, such as: oil, acrylic, and gouache painting, drawing, digital art, and graphic design. Inspired by her many professors, Danielle has spent the majority of her focus commissioning and selling portraits, oil paintings and illustrations. She strives to continue to grow as an artist, and create work that brings joy and positivity to those who view it.

Acknowledgements, thank yous, and all that fancy stuff . . .

. . . because I've been dreaming of doing something for the majority of my life, and I've had enough time to choose the most perfectly wonderful people I could ever wish for to make that dream a beautiful reality.

And I find myself reflecting on where it all began . . .

At the age of 16, I sat at my desk, soaking in everything possible from my Creative Writing Instructor at our local high school. I had always loved learning, and during this year, I had discovered that writing was my thing, my passion! It filled me with joy and peace and wonder. Putting pen to paper offered me the opportunity to be, to do, to dream, and to explore ALL that my imagination could offer. It was during that year of my life that so many major changes occurred, and I believe writing helped me survive the most difficult moments.

I distinctly remember the day that a graded paper was plopped on my desk, with the usual happy smile from Mr. ??? . . . How I wish I could recall his name! For the life of me, I cannot, but I will never forget how he made me feel . . . He stood, I believe just to see my reaction . . . I remember looking at him and seeing the most genuine smile cross his face, he was always such a cheerful man, which may have been partly why I enjoyed coming to his class so much each day, but today felt a little differently.

This "graded paper," which at one time had been nothing more than blank sheets of white typing paper, was now a small illustrated book, if you will. (If I close my eyes, I can still feel the texture of those pages in my fingers.) I had taken those sheets and created a mini-masterpiece as I plunked away on my fancy typewriter adding illustrations of colored pencil here and there. It may have appeared to be nothing more than a few papers joined together—staple in the left-hand corner with a dabble of sketches and scribbles—seeming to be nothing all that special.

For me, it was so much more! I had poured my heart into those pages, I had spent countless hours developing the characters, the story, the environment and setting, the perfect message . . .

In that moment, pure excitement rushed through my body!

To be fair, I ought to pause here to mention I had received my fair share of "A" grades (that's what being a "people-pleaser" will do for you), but, in all of those A papers, never had I seen this! There before me, lay my little book, with a note at the top, and next to it (in Red Ink, I might add) was a big, fat A+++!!! Yep, that's right! A+++!!! Count 'em: 1-2-3!!! Holy Smokes!!! I didn't even know that was a possible grade!!!

What do you think I did? Well, naturally I held that paper to my chest hugging it and soaking it all in. I had created something I loved and there was another human in this world who was moved by that creation. In that very moment, I knew that I was born to share messages with others . . . nothing delighted me the way that writing could.

Fast forward 32+ years . . .

The very first copy of The Glitter Keeper was handed to me . . . tears started stinging at my eyes, and—you guessed it! I reacted in much the same way. I hugged that book to my chest, overcome with a flood of emotions . . . another magical moment had just come to pass. The dream I had allowed to stay tucked away for soooooo long was now in my hands and ready to be shared with the world! Holy Hay Buckets! It was REAL!

This time, however, I did not accomplish the feat on my own. I surrounded myself with the VERY BEST!!! There are many things I've learned in all these years, and quite possibly one of the most important is that We are Better Together!

For years and years, I've secretly watched artists, looking for just the right fit. Then, I met Miss Dani Powell! Her style was everything I had wished for and she had a way of listening to my visions and helping those visions spring to life on the pages! I had a picture in my head of Trudy, and Dani nailed it! I seriously cried tears when I saw the first sketch of Trudy . . . she was so perfect! She was everything I had imagined! Danielle, I can never thank you enough for the time and love you've put into The Glitter Keeper. YOU were my first dream come true with this story. I love you to pieces, Sweet Girl! The world is at your fingertips and I cannot wait to see what you do with your beautiful gifts and talents! One thing is for sure—you will make this world sparkle and shine!

Next, I went to the person that knew my "writing voice" better than anyone: my dear friend, Jerusha Smith. This lady is The World's BEST Editor! She's edited many things for me over the years, but I think we would both agree that living life with Trudy for the past few months has been the ultimate! Who knows what will be coming next?!?! Jerusha picked me up time and again as I struggled to share what was in my heart and work through giving Trudy her voice. Jerusha, I love and adore you and owe you the world!!! Thank you, My Friend, for standing by my side and laughing with me through it all! And maybe, just maybe, one day, we'll spot an "icecycle" or a Bleeding Heart flower and bust out in laughter with no one having a clue, except us! You are a joy and a blessing to me! Thank you for walking this journey of ups and downs with me!

And just when all seemed hopeless . . .

When I was certain that I was crazy to believe I could really make this all happen, with one obstacle after another jumping in the way, friends by the dozens knew just when to call, just when to reach out, just when to offer an encouraging word, just when to remind me to keep digging, and that the diamonds were right ahead of me if I just wouldn't put that shovel down. Thank you for encouraging me to not give up! For all of the people who've believed in me and pushed me to be my very best; for those who helped me break down my walls and rebuild; for those who stood by my side cheering me on, truly celebrating with me, as I DID THIS—I love and appreciate you!

And finally to Tyler Penner . . .

You were the last puzzle piece. You have been an absolute gift from God to me! Thank you for all the coffee-house visits, for putting up with my endless, "Do you think we can move that . . . add another swirly here and a heart there . . . ohhhh, and glitter . . . we need MORE GLITTER . . . can you possibly add this and change that font and, and, and . . ." And each time, you'd reply, with your darling smile, "Yeah, no problem!" Before I knew it, it was better than I had dreamed! Your expertise in formatting and publication has been exactly what I needed! And the day you handed me my first copy of The Glitter Keeper . . . WOW!!! YOU have gone above and beyond all that I could have ever wished and hoped for . . . YOU rescued my dream and helped make it what it is today. My heart is forever grateful to you!!! Get ready, 'cause there is so much more in me, and YOU will always be my go-to!!!

Thank you all for helping me to find joy in the journey!!!

.

Made in the USA
Middletown, DE
22 December 2020